Dreams in White Coats: Dr. Olivia's Odyssey through Ten Healing Realms

Wilfred Pool

Copyright © 2024 Wilfred Pool

All rights reserved.

ISBN:

DEDICATION

To My Wife, Children, AI and Pet.

CONTENTS

	Acknowledgments	i
1	A Call to Duty	Pg 1
2	Echoes of Betrayal	Pg 3
3	The Tangled Web	Pg 7
4	Beneath the Surface	Pg 10
5	Shadows of Doubt	Pg 14
6	The Silent Advocate	Pg 17
7	Fractured Alliances	Pg 20
8	Breaking Point	Pg 23
9	Shadows of Redemption	Pg 26
10	A Healing Light	Pg 29

ACKNOWLEDGMENTS

I would like to express my sincere gratitude to ChatGPT for its invaluable assistance in the creation of this book. The collaboration with ChatGPT has proven to be an essential and enriching aspect of the writing process, contributing to the development and refinement of ideas. Its ability to generate creative and insightful content has significantly enhanced the overall quality of this work. I extend my appreciation to ChatGPT for being an exceptional writing partner and an integral part of bringing this book to fruition.

I extend my heartfelt appreciation to Amazon for providing a platform to showcase and sell my book. The vast reach and user-friendly interface of the Amazon platform have played a pivotal role in making my work accessible to a wide audience. I am grateful for the seamless publishing and distribution services that Amazon offers, allowing my book to find its way into the hands of readers around the world. The support and opportunities provided by Amazon have been instrumental in the success of my book, and I am truly thankful for the partnership

1 A CALL TO DUTY

The sterile hospital air hummed with urgency as Dr. Olivia Sterling Turner, her scrubs adorned with the telltale signs of a seasoned surgeon, briskly navigated the labyrinthine corridors of St. Mercy Hospital. Her steps were purposeful, each one carrying the weight of years of medical experience and a reputation for unparalleled surgical skill. The overhead announcement system crackled to life, the disembodied voice delivering a message that sent a ripple of tension through the bustling hospital. "Code Blue, Emergency Room, Trauma Bay 1." Olivia Sterling's heart quickened, and without hesitation, she altered her course towards the designated location. A sense of duty, ingrained through years of medical training, propelled her forward. As she arrived at the trauma bay, a chaotic scene unfolded before her. The victim of a horrific car accident lay on the gurney, surrounded by a team of frenzied medical professionals. The air buzzed with urgency as they worked together to stabilize the patient. Olivia Sterling, accustomed to the organized chaos of emergency situations, seamlessly joined the effort. The trauma bay became a theater of controlled chaos, with medical instruments clattering and the rhythmic beeping of machines in the background. Olivia Sterling's hands moved with a precision that spoke of countless surgeries, her mind fully immersed in the delicate dance between life and death. As the crisis began to abate, Olivia Sterling took a step back, her eyes fixed on the patient whose life hung in the balance. The room, moments ago filled with frenetic energy, now settled into a tense calm. It was then that Olivia Sterling noticed a familiar face among the onlookers — a nurse who had once been a colleague and a confidante. With a quick exchange of glances, the nurse communicated the unspoken, and Olivia Sterling's heart sank. This was no ordinary emergency. The patient on the

Dreams in White Coats:

Dr. Olivia's Odyssey through Ten Healing Realms

gurney, battered and bruised, was more than a victim of circumstance. This case was intricately linked to Olivia Sterling's past, dredging up memories she had long sought to bury. As the patient was wheeled away for further treatment, Olivia Sterling's mind raced. The ghost of a shadowy figure from her past lingered in the recesses of her memory. A face she thought she had left behind, a name etched into the corridors of time — Dr. Richard Harrington. Richard, a brilliant but morally questionable surgeon, had once been Olivia Sterling's mentor. The echoes of their shared history reverberated in the sterile walls of the hospital. It was under his guidance that Olivia Sterling had honed her surgical skills, but the cost had been steep — a compromise of ethical principles that had eventually driven her to distance herself from her once-respected mentor. The unexpected reappearance of Richard in this dire emergency triggered a cascade of emotions within Olivia Sterling. She was torn between the call of duty and the unresolved conflicts of her past. The patient's life now rested in the hands of a medical team, but Olivia Sterling's internal struggle had just begun. As the trauma bay slowly emptied, Olivia Sterling retreated to her office, a small sanctuary where the harsh fluorescent lights couldn't pierce the veil of her contemplation. Her hands trembled as she dialed a number she had long since removed from her contacts, a number belonging to the enigmatic figure of Richard Harrington. The line rang, each tone echoing the uncertainty that gripped Olivia Sterling's heart. After several anxious moments, a voice answered, low and authoritative, "Olivia Sterling, I knew this day would come." The past, dormant for years, had resurfaced, thrusting Olivia Sterling into a precarious situation where duty and personal history collided. The call to duty had summoned her, but the shadows of her past now demanded acknowledgment, and Olivia Sterling knew that to move forward, she had to confront the ghosts that lingered in the corridors of her memory. As the conversation with Richard unfolded, Olivia Sterling's journey into the heart of her past began, setting the stage for a series of challenges that would test not only her surgical prowess but also the very fabric of her moral compass. The shadows, once dismissed, now loomed large, casting an ominous pall over the future that awaited Dr. Olivia Sterling Turner.

2 ECHOES OF BETRAYAL

The dimly lit room echoed with the soft hum of medical equipment, creating an atmosphere of sterile detachment. Dr. Olivia Sterling Hartley, a seasoned psychiatrist with an air of professionalism, sat behind her desk, her gaze fixed on the case file before her. The clock on the wall ticked away, marking the passing of time as she reviewed the details of her newest patient, a mystery wrapped in the enigma of her own history. Olivia Sterling had always prided herself on maintaining emotional distance from her patients, a skill honed through years of practice. However, this case was different. The name on the file brought back a flood of memories, a haunting reminder of a betrayal that had left scars on her soul. Vanessa Morgan, the patient in question, was a living echo of the past, a shadow that had come back to haunt Olivia Sterling. As Olivia Sterling delved into Vanessa's file, she couldn't shake the feeling that this was more than a mere coincidence. The universe had an uncanny way of playing tricks, and here she was, face to face with a name she had long tried to bury in the recesses of her mind. Vanessa's history revealed a troubled past, marked by trauma and a series of failed therapeutic interventions. Olivia Sterling sighed, realizing that she was stepping into a delicate and intricate dance, one that required both professional acumen and emotional resilience. With a deep breath, Olivia Sterling opened the door to the consultation room, where Vanessa awaited. The room was adorned with soothing colors and comfortable furniture, an intentional design to foster a sense of calm. Vanessa sat on the plush chair, her eyes fixed on the floor. As Olivia Sterling took her seat opposite her, the air in the room seemed to thicken with unspoken tension. "Good afternoon, Vanessa. I'm Dr. Olivia Sterling Hartley," Olivia Sterling began, her voice measured and calm. "I've had the chance

Dreams in White Coats:

Dr. Olivia's Odyssey through Ten Healing Realms

to review your file, but I would like to hear your story from your own perspective. Take your time." Vanessa looked up, her eyes clouded with a mixture of apprehension and sadness. She began to recount her troubled journey, the narrative unfolding like a dark tapestry of pain and betrayal. Olivia Sterling listened intently, her clinical instincts alert while her own emotions lurked beneath the surface, threatening to surface like dormant monsters. As Vanessa spoke, Olivia Sterling couldn't help but draw parallels between the young woman before her and the haunting memories of her own past. The echoes of betrayal resonated in Vanessa's words, triggering suppressed emotions within Olivia Sterling. It was a delicate dance on the precipice of her own vulnerabilities, a test of her ability to separate personal history from professional duty. Days turned into weeks as Olivia Sterling embarked on the arduous task of guiding Vanessa through the labyrinth of her traumas. Each session became a journey into the recesses of the human psyche, a dance of vulnerability and strength. Olivia Sterling found herself grappling with the ghosts of her past, wrestling with the shadows that threatened to engulf her. In the quiet moments between sessions, Olivia Sterling would sit alone in her office, staring at the walls that seemed to close in on her. The weight of her own history pressed upon her shoulders, threatening to break the carefully constructed façade of professionalism. She knew she couldn't let her past dictate the course of Vanessa's therapy, but the echoes of betrayal were relentless, whispering in the corners of her mind. One evening, as the sun dipped below the horizon, casting long shadows across the city, Olivia Sterling received an unexpected phone call. The voice on the other end sent shivers down her spine – a voice she hadn't heard in years, a voice that carried the weight of secrets and shattered trust. "Olivia Sterling, it's me. Richard." The name hung in the air, a specter from the past. Richard, the one whose betrayal had set Olivia Sterling on a path of healing and self-discovery. The wounds he had inflicted were scars now, but the sudden reappearance of his voice tore open old wounds, releasing a flood of emotions she thought she had buried deep. "Why are you calling, Richard?" Olivia Sterling's voice was steady, a façade of composure masking the turmoil within. "I heard about your new patient, Vanessa. You need to be careful, Olivia Sterling. You know how delicate the threads of the past can be," Richard warned, his tone a chilling reminder of the tangled history they shared. Olivia Sterling's mind raced as she grappled with the intrusion of her past into her present. Richard's words carried a cryptic weight, a warning that echoed through the corridors of her consciousness. Was Vanessa merely

Dreams in White Coats:

Dr. Olivia's Odyssey through Ten Healing Realms

a patient, or was she a pawn in a game of retribution orchestrated by the ghost of betrayal? Determined to maintain her professional integrity, Olivia Sterling returned to her sessions with Vanessa, a renewed sense of purpose guiding her. The revelations about her past had added layers to the therapeutic process, turning it into a dual journey of healing – both for Vanessa and for Olivia Sterling herself. The echoes of betrayal reverberated through the sessions, intertwining the fates of therapist and patient. As Vanessa peeled away the layers of her trauma, Olivia Sterling found herself confronting her own demons, the shadows of a past she had tried so hard to escape. The line between healer and the one in need of healing blurred, creating a surreal dance of vulnerability and strength. In the midst of this intricate dance, Olivia Sterling discovered an unexpected ally in Vanessa. The young woman's resilience and determination to overcome her past mirrored Olivia Sterling's own journey. They became partners in a quest for redemption, each step forward a triumph over the shadows that threatened to engulf them. The therapy sessions became a crucible of transformation, a space where the echoes of betrayal could be reshaped into a narrative of resilience and healing. Olivia Sterling guided Vanessa through the labyrinth of her trauma, offering insights born from her own struggles. In turn, Vanessa became a mirror reflecting Olivia Sterling's own journey, a reminder that healing was a reciprocal process. As the weeks turned into months, the therapeutic alliance between Olivia Sterling and Vanessa deepened. The walls that had separated them crumbled, giving way to a shared understanding that transcended the traditional roles of therapist and patient. In the crucible of therapy, Olivia Sterling found solace in the act of healing others, realizing that the key to her own redemption lay in helping Vanessa reclaim her own narrative. One day, as the sun dipped below the horizon, casting a warm glow across the city, Olivia Sterling and Vanessa sat in a moment of shared silence. The air was thick with the unspoken – a silent acknowledgment of the journey they had undertaken together. The echoes of betrayal lingered, but they were no longer harbingers of pain. Instead, they had become stepping stones on a path of transformation. In the quiet of that moment, Olivia Sterling realized that the dance with her own shadows had not ended; rather, it had evolved into a graceful ballet of resilience and redemption. The therapeutic journey with Vanessa had become a catalyst for Olivia Sterling's own healing, a testament to the profound connection between past wounds and the possibility of renewal. As the chapter of Vanessa's therapy drew to a close, Olivia Sterling felt a sense of accomplishment

Dreams in White Coats:

Dr. Olivia's Odyssey through Ten Healing Realms

and closure. The echoes of betrayal, once haunting specters, had transformed into whispers of strength and triumph. The therapeutic process had become a two-way street, a dance of healing that transcended the boundaries of time and pain. As Vanessa stepped out into the world, carrying the tools of resilience and self-discovery, Olivia Sterling remained in her office, reflecting on the transformative power of the therapeutic relationship. The shadows of her past, while not completely erased, had taken on a softer hue, no longer looming as insurmountable obstacles. The weight that Olivia Sterling had carried for so long began to lift, replaced by a newfound sense of purpose and closure. In the days that followed Vanessa's departure, Olivia Sterling found herself revisiting the fragments of her own history, examining them with a fresh perspective. The unexpected reunion with Richard, the cryptic warnings he had imparted, and the subsequent therapeutic journey with Vanessa had all become interconnected threads weaving a complex tapestry of resilience and redemption. The therapeutic process had not only facilitated Vanessa's healing but had also unearthed dormant aspects of Olivia Sterling's own strength. The echoes of betrayal, once haunting, had now become catalysts for growth and self-discovery. Olivia Sterling realized that the ghosts of her past were not to be feared but acknowledged as integral parts of her narrative. As she navigated the delicate balance between professional duty and personal demons, Olivia Sterling began to see the value in vulnerability. Sharing fragments of her own story with Vanessa had not compromised the therapeutic alliance; instead, it had strengthened the connection between them. The wall between therapist and patient had crumbled, giving way to a mutual understanding that transcended traditional boundaries.

3 THE TANGLED WEB

The hospital hummed with the usual orchestrated chaos, the symphony of medical professionals working tirelessly to provide care. Dr. Olivia Sterling Hartley navigated the corridors with the ease of familiarity, her white coat billowing behind her as she moved from one patient to another. The echoes of her own healing journey lingered in the background, a subtle reminder of the resilience forged through personal trials. However, the tranquility of the hospital setting was soon shattered by a series of unusual cases that landed on Olivia Sterling's desk. Patients exhibiting mysterious symptoms, unexplained medical anomalies, and a rising tide of discontent among the hospital staff hinted at an undercurrent of turmoil. Olivia Sterling, attuned to the subtle shifts in the hospital's dynamics, sensed that something far more sinister lurked beneath the surface. As a seasoned psychiatrist, Olivia Sterling's initial inclination was to focus on the mental health aspect of these cases. Were these symptoms manifestations of underlying psychological distress? But as the number of cases multiplied, she couldn't ignore the pervasive sense that there was more to the story than met the eye. The first red flag waved when Olivia Sterling encountered Mrs. Eleanor Thompson, a patient admitted with a sudden onset of neurological symptoms that defied conventional diagnosis. As Olivia Sterling delved into Mrs. Thompson's medical history, she discovered a pattern—a pattern that extended beyond the confines of individual cases. The thread connecting these cases led Olivia Sterling into a labyrinth of intrigue, a tangled web of deceit and corruption that threatened to compromise patient care. It became evident that a network of individuals, driven by motives still unclear, was manipulating the very fabric of the hospital's operations. The more Olivia Sterling dug into the mysteries, the deeper she found

Dreams in White Coats:

Dr. Olivia's Odyssey through Ten Healing Realms

herself entangled in the web. She questioned colleagues discreetly, pored over medical records, and sought counsel from trusted allies. It became apparent that these anomalies weren't isolated incidents but part of a larger scheme to exploit the vulnerabilities within the hospital's infrastructure. In her pursuit of truth, Olivia Sterling faced resistance from unexpected quarters. Colleagues who had once been allies seemed hesitant to speak openly. Whispers of a clandestine power dynamic circulated, leaving Olivia Sterling with a growing sense of isolation. The tangled web threatened not only the integrity of patient care but also the foundations of trust that held the medical community together. Determined to unravel the mysteries, Olivia Sterling turned to Marcus Turner, an investigative journalist and an old friend. Together, they delved into the shadows, connecting dots that revealed a pattern of kickbacks, manipulated diagnoses, and compromised patient well-being. The hospital, once a sanctuary of healing, had become a battleground where ethics clashed with greed. As Olivia Sterling peeled away the layers of deception, she found herself confronting a moral dilemma. Exposing the truth would undoubtedly tarnish the reputation of the institution she had dedicated her career to. Yet, to turn a blind eye would mean betraying the very principles that defined her as a healer. The weight of responsibility pressed upon her shoulders as she grappled with the consequences of her pursuit of justice. The web of corruption extended beyond the hospital walls, reaching into the corridors of power that governed the medical community. Olivia Sterling's reputation, once a pillar of trust, now hung in the balance. The tangled web threatened to ensnare her, not just as an investigator but as a compassionate healer caught in the crossfire of deceit. Late one evening, as Olivia Sterling poured over stacks of documents in her dimly lit office, she received an anonymous message. The words were cryptic, hinting at the dangers she faced in her quest for truth. The sender urged caution, reminding her that the web of corruption extended its tendrils into unexpected places. Fear rippled through Olivia Sterling, not for herself but for the patients who depended on the hospital for care. The anonymous warning fueled her determination to expose the truth, regardless of the personal cost. With Marcus by her side, she delved deeper, navigating the labyrinth of deceit with a steely resolve. The tension within the hospital escalated as whispers of an internal investigation spread. Colleagues, once reticent to share information, now began to confide in Olivia Sterling. The web of corruption, it seemed, had ensnared not only the hospital administrators but also individuals within the medical staff. Loyalties were tested, and

Dreams in White Coats:

Dr. Olivia's Odyssey through Ten Healing Realms

alliances shifted as the truth threatened to unravel. In a clandestine meeting with Marcus, Olivia Sterling discovered a key piece of evidence that could expose the entire network of corruption. A ledger, meticulously maintained by a whistleblower within the hospital, documented the flow of illicit funds and the names of those complicit in the scheme. Armed with this damning evidence, Olivia Sterling and Marcus faced a critical decision—expose the truth immediately or gather more evidence to ensure an airtight case. The web tightened around them as they tiptoed through the shadows, always aware of the eyes watching from the periphery. Olivia Sterling's dedication to her patients, combined with Marcus's investigative prowess, became a beacon of hope in the face of pervasive deceit. The hospital, once a symbol of healing, now stood at the precipice of a reckoning. As Olivia Sterling prepared to unveil the evidence, a storm of uncertainty loomed on the horizon. The tangled web threatened to resist their efforts, retaliating with a force that could jeopardize not only Olivia Sterling's career but the very foundations of the medical institution she sought to protect. The final chapter of this harrowing saga awaited, and the resolution would determine the fate of not only the hospital but also the principles that guided Olivia Sterling's life and profession.

4 BENEATH THE SURFACE

The hospital corridors echoed with a renewed sense of anticipation. Olivia Sterling found herself at the epicenter of a groundbreaking medical discovery that promised to reshape the landscape of scientific advancement. Her research, focused on unraveling the mysteries of a rare neurological condition, had garnered attention far beyond the confines of her institution. Accolades poured in from prestigious medical journals, conferences extended invitations for her to present, and colleagues hailed Olivia Sterling as a pioneer in the field. As the spotlight intensified, she became a symbol of progress, the embodiment of the relentless pursuit of knowledge within the medical community. Yet, beneath the surface of this seemingly triumphant narrative, Olivia Sterling sensed the weight of an unspoken truth. The euphoria of professional success was tinged with an underlying unease. The research that had catapulted her into the forefront of scientific acclaim held a darker secret, a moral dilemma buried deep within the corridors of medical ethics. The breakthrough lay in a novel treatment for the neurological condition, a treatment that showed unprecedented efficacy in initial trials. Patients who had once faced debilitating symptoms now experienced remarkable improvement, their lives transformed by Olivia Sterling's groundbreaking research. However, as the accolades mounted, so did Olivia Sterling's awareness of the ethical implications of her discovery. The treatment, while undeniably effective, came at a cost—one that raised profound questions about the boundaries of medical experimentation and the potential exploitation of vulnerable patients. In the hallowed halls of scientific progress, Olivia Sterling found herself wrestling with the age-old tension between professional success and the well-being of her patients. The more she delved into the ethical complexities, the more she realized the

Dreams in White Coats:

Dr. Olivia's Odyssey through Ten Healing Realms

precarious nature of the path she had embarked upon. Late one night, as she pored over the data in her office, Olivia Sterling received a call from Dr. Rebecca Martinez, a respected bioethicist and longtime mentor. Rebecca's voice, tinged with concern, cut through the silence of Olivia Sterling's contemplation. "Olivia Sterling, your research is groundbreaking, there's no denying that. But I urge you to consider the ethical implications. We must ensure that progress doesn't come at the expense of human dignity and the principles that guide our profession," Rebecca advised, her words echoing in the dimly lit room. The conversation with Rebecca ignited a spark of introspection within Olivia Sterling. She began to scrutinize her own motivations and the potential consequences of her research. The faces of the patients who had benefitted from the treatment flashed before her eyes, their stories a testament to the potential for positive change. Yet, as she delved deeper, Olivia Sterling couldn't ignore the nagging question—what were the long-term effects of the treatment? The rush to embrace progress had overshadowed the need for thorough scrutiny. An ethical dilemma unfurled before her, a choice between professional acclaim and the obligation to safeguard the well-being of her patients. In the following weeks, Olivia Sterling immersed herself in a delicate dance between scientific ambition and moral responsibility. The accolades continued to pour in, but a growing sense of internal conflict accompanied each accolade. The weight of the ethical dilemma pressed upon her, a constant reminder that progress, when not guided by ethical considerations, could become a double-edged sword. The turning point came when Olivia Sterling encountered a patient, Sophia Rodriguez, whose condition had deteriorated despite initially positive responses to the treatment. As Olivia Sterling stood at Sophia's bedside, the gravity of her responsibilities as a healer and researcher converged. The ethical dilemma, once an abstract concept, now manifested in the frail form of a patient who trusted her expertise. Olivia Sterling embarked on a journey of introspection, consulting with colleagues, seeking the guidance of ethics committees, and engaging in conversations with patients who had participated in the trials. The more perspectives she gathered, the clearer the ethical landscape became. The treatment, while transformative for some, carried risks and uncertainties that demanded transparency and informed consent. In a pivotal meeting with hospital administrators and the ethics committee, Olivia Sterling presented her findings and proposed a framework for more stringent ethical oversight. She advocated for transparency in communicating the potential risks to patients and

Dreams in White Coats:

Dr. Olivia's Odyssey through Ten Healing Realms

emphasized the importance of ongoing monitoring to ensure the long-term safety and efficacy of the treatment. The decision to prioritize ethics over unchecked progress was met with resistance. Some saw it as a hindrance to innovation, while others questioned the need for additional bureaucratic hurdles. Olivia Sterling, however, stood firm in her conviction that the pursuit of knowledge should not compromise the fundamental principles of patient care. As the ethical framework gained acceptance, Olivia Sterling faced the consequences of her choices. The accolades that once showered her now dwindled, and whispers of skepticism circulated within the scientific community. Olivia Sterling, however, found solace in the knowledge that her research, now guided by a commitment to ethical integrity, would stand the test of time. The hospital, once again the stage for a transformative journey, became a beacon of ethical progress in the field of medical research. Olivia Sterling's story, intertwined with the ethical complexities of scientific advancement, served as a cautionary tale for a profession often enamored with the allure of discovery. Beneath the surface of professional success, Olivia Sterling discovered a reservoir of resilience and moral fortitude. The shadows of the ethical dilemma, while not completely dispelled, became a source of enlightenment rather than darkness. Olivia Sterling continued her work, not as a pioneer blinded by ambition, but as a compassionate healer committed to advancing knowledge within the boundaries of ethical responsibility. The chapter of scientific discovery had not ended, but it had evolved into a narrative of balance—a delicate dance between progress and ethical considerations. As Olivia Sterling navigated the treacherous waters of medical ethics, she became a guiding light for those who dared to venture into the uncharted territories of scientific exploration. The story of "Beneath the Surface" unfolded, a testament to the enduring interplay between professional success and the unwavering commitment to the well-being of humanity.

5 SHADOWS OF DOUBT

The hospital, once a bastion of healing and progress, found itself shrouded in an ominous cloud. A sudden influx of patients, each presenting with mysterious and debilitating symptoms, sent shockwaves through the medical community. Olivia Sterling, ever-committed to her role as a healer, was thrust into a race against time to unravel the medical mystery that threatened not only the well-being of the patients but also the reputation of the institution she held dear. The whispers of doubt reverberated through the hospital corridors as colleagues exchanged concerned glances. The once-celebrated researcher, whose ethical considerations had reshaped the landscape of medical advancement, now faced the daunting challenge of solving a perplexing medical puzzle. The shadows of doubt cast their long fingers, pointing not only at the mysterious symptoms afflicting the patients but also at Olivia Sterling's abilities as a diagnostician. As the cases multiplied, Olivia Sterling delved into the intricate details of each patient's medical history, searching for commonalities, connections, and potential triggers. The pressure mounted with each passing day, the weight of responsibility pressing upon her shoulders. The hospital's reputation, once sterling, now hung in the balance. The patients, afflicted by symptoms that defied conventional diagnosis, became a collective enigma. Olivia Sterling, surrounded by uncertainty, sought counsel from colleagues, specialists, and experts in various fields. However, the answers remained elusive, hidden beneath layers of complexity that seemed impenetrable. In the midst of the medical turmoil, Olivia Sterling confronted her own insecurities. The echoes of doubt whispered in the recesses of her mind, questioning her capabilities as a healer. The once-confident psychiatrist found herself navigating uncharted waters, grappling with a sense of

Dreams in White Coats:

Dr. Olivia's Odyssey through Ten Healing Realms

vulnerability that threatened to erode the foundation of her professional identity. Late nights in the hospital became a solitary journey of introspection for Olivia Sterling. The walls of her office, once adorned with accolades and certificates, now closed in on her, echoing the doubts that crept into her consciousness. The weight of expectation, both self-imposed and external, became a heavy burden that threatened to drown her in a sea of uncertainty. In the quiet moments between patient consultations and research endeavors, Olivia Sterling found solace in unexpected places. A conversation with a nurse who had weathered similar storms, the reassuring words of a long-time mentor, and the shared humanity of her colleagues all served as beacons of light in the shadows of doubt. As Olivia Sterling continued her relentless pursuit of answers, she discovered that sometimes the greatest healing came from acknowledging one's vulnerabilities. The patients, too, became allies in the journey, their resilience inspiring her to press on despite the uncertainties that surrounded them. The medical mystery, like a labyrinth with ever-shifting walls, demanded creative thinking and unconventional approaches. Olivia Sterling, embracing her role as both investigator and healer, collaborated with specialists from diverse fields—neurology, infectious diseases, environmental health—to cast a wider net in the search for solutions. The breakthrough, when it came, was not heralded by trumpets or accolades. Instead, it unfolded quietly, like a dawn breaking after a long night of uncertainty. Through meticulous research, collaboration, and a willingness to entertain unconventional hypotheses, the elusive commonality among the patients began to emerge. A seemingly innocuous environmental factor, overlooked in the initial assessments, was identified as the potential trigger for the mysterious symptoms. The discovery not only shed light on the medical puzzle but also lifted the shadow of doubt that had hung over Olivia Sterling's abilities. As the hospital rallied to address the environmental concern and implement necessary measures, Olivia Sterling found herself standing at the intersection of humility and resilience. The journey through the shadows of doubt had tested her mettle, revealing that strength could be found not only in unwavering confidence but also in the courage to acknowledge uncertainty. The hospital's reputation, tarnished but not irreparably damaged, began to recover. Colleagues who had hesitated to lend support now extended gestures of solidarity. The medical community, recognizing the challenges inherent in navigating complex medical mysteries, rallied around Olivia Sterling, acknowledging the shared vulnerability that

Dreams in White Coats:

Dr. Olivia's Odyssey through Ten Healing Realms

defined their profession. In the aftermath of the crisis, Olivia Sterling reflected on the profound lessons learned during this tumultuous chapter. She realized that healing, both for patients and for herself, came not only from the triumphs but also from the acknowledgment of imperfections and the resilience to confront doubts head-on. As the hospital returned to a semblance of normalcy, Olivia Sterling emerged from the shadows of doubt with a newfound wisdom. The patients, whose collective mystery had cast a pall over the institution, became living testaments to the interconnectedness of humanity. The hospital, weathered but resilient, stood as a symbol of the enduring spirit that thrives even in the face of uncertainty. The shadows of doubt, once menacing, had become stepping stones on Olivia Sterling's journey of growth and self-discovery. The chapter, though challenging, had imparted invaluable insights that would resonate throughout her career as a healer and researcher. As Olivia Sterling embraced the ongoing dance between triumphs and vulnerabilities, she understood that the greatest healing often emerged from the shadows where doubt and resilience converged.

6 THE SILENT ADVOCATE

The hospital, though emerging from the shadows of doubt, became the stage for a new and challenging drama. Olivia Sterling found herself unwittingly thrust into the role of an advocate for a patient silenced by a system that prioritized power over compassion. As she delved into the complexities of the patient's case, Olivia Sterling discovered a web of corruption and indifference that reached deep into the heart of the medical establishment. It all began with Mrs. Evelyn Rodriguez, a middle-aged woman whose quiet demeanor hid a story of pain and neglect. Olivia Sterling, with her heightened sensitivity to the struggles of those in her care, noticed that Mrs. Rodriguez's medical concerns were consistently dismissed by her primary physician. The patient's pleas for a thorough examination were met with condescension and indifference, revealing a stark contrast to the compassionate care that should define the medical profession. Digging deeper into Mrs. Rodriguez's medical history, Olivia Sterling uncovered a disturbing pattern of negligence and systemic failures. The hospital, it seemed, was plagued by a culture that prioritized expediency over patient advocacy, where the voices of the vulnerable were drowned out by the bureaucratic machinery. The realization ignited a fire within Olivia Sterling—a determination to be the voice for those silenced by a callous system. She embarked on a journey to unravel the layers of neglect surrounding Mrs. Rodriguez's case, facing formidable adversaries within the medical establishment who sought to maintain the status quo. Olivia Sterling's quest for justice faced immediate resistance. Colleagues who had once celebrated her ethical considerations now distanced themselves, wary of the disruptive force she threatened to become. The hospital administrators, protective of their reputation, dismissed her concerns as unfounded and disruptive.

Dreams in White Coats:

Dr. Olivia's Odyssey through Ten Healing Realms

Undeterred, Olivia Sterling sought counsel from Dr. Rebecca Martinez, the bioethicist whose wisdom had guided her through previous challenges. Rebecca, recognizing the importance of advocating for the vulnerable, urged Olivia Sterling to become the voice that echoed in the corridors of power. As Olivia Sterling navigated the bureaucratic hurdles, she discovered that Mrs. Rodriguez's case was not isolated. There were others, silent victims of a system that valued efficiency over empathy. The echoes of injustice reverberated within the hospital's walls, casting a long shadow over the very principles that should define medical care. The turning point came when Olivia Sterling unearthed evidence of deliberate negligence within the hospital. Documents concealed in the maze of bureaucracy revealed a pattern of willful ignorance, where the concerns of patients like Mrs. Rodriguez were dismissed to protect the interests of those in power. Armed with irrefutable evidence, Olivia Sterling confronted the hospital administrators, demanding accountability and transparency. The shadows of corruption, once concealed, now loomed large as the hospital faced the prospect of public scrutiny. Olivia Sterling, unwittingly transformed into a force for change, stood resolute in her commitment to justice. The battle to expose the truth intensified as Olivia Sterling faced personal and professional backlash. Colleagues whispered accusations of betrayal, and administrators wielded their influence to tarnish her reputation. Olivia Sterling, however, drew strength from the silent voices of the neglected patients, realizing that her advocacy was not just for Mrs. Rodriguez but for every individual who had been failed by a broken system. In the midst of the storm, Olivia Sterling found unexpected allies—nurses, support staff, and even a few courageous physicians who had witnessed the injustices but remained silent out of fear. Together, they formed a coalition of change, challenging the entrenched powers that had perpetuated a culture of neglect within the hospital. The battle for justice extended beyond the confines of the hospital. Olivia Sterling sought the support of patient advocacy groups, legal experts, and the media to shine a spotlight on the pervasive issues plaguing the medical establishment. The silent advocate became a rallying cry for systemic change, a call to dismantle the shadows of corruption that lurked within the very heart of healthcare. As the investigation unfolded, the hospital administrators were forced to confront the undeniable truth. The evidence, now laid bare for all to see, painted a damning picture of neglect and indifference. The silent voices of the neglected patients became a roar, echoing through the hallways of power. The aftermath brought both triumph and

Dreams in White Coats:

Dr. Olivia's Odyssey through Ten Healing Realms

tragedy. The hospital, once resistant to change, was compelled to reevaluate its practices and instigate reforms to prioritize patient advocacy. Olivia Sterling, though vindicated, bore the scars of the battle. The personal toll of standing against the shadows of corruption lingered, a reminder of the sacrifices made in the pursuit of justice. As the silent advocate, Olivia Sterling's journey became a beacon of inspiration for those within and beyond the medical community. Patient advocacy groups hailed her as a hero, and the media portrayed her as a symbol of resilience against institutional indifference. The shadows she had faced now served as a testament to the enduring power of a single voice determined to bring about change. In the quiet aftermath of the battle, Olivia Sterling reflected on the transformative nature of her journey. The silent advocate had found her voice, not in the echoes of applause but in the resolute commitment to the principles that defined her as a healer. The shadows of corruption, while formidable, had ultimately crumbled in the face of unwavering determination and the collective outcry for justice. As Olivia Sterling continued her work, she remained vigilant against the insidious shadows that threatened to creep back. The silent advocate, now a symbol of resilience, stood as a reminder that the pursuit of justice was an ongoing battle—one that required vigilance, courage, and an unwavering commitment to the well-being of those in her care.

7 FRACTURED ALLIANCES

The hospital, still reeling from the echoes of the silent advocate's crusade, found itself plunged into a new crisis—one that tested the very fabric of professional and personal alliances. The revelation of a respected colleague's involvement in a medical scandal sent shockwaves through the medical community, casting shadows of doubt that threatened to engulf even the most steadfast bonds. Dr. Lawrence Harris, a seasoned physician and once a trusted ally, stood accused of ethical misconduct that rocked the foundations of the hospital. The scandal, a stark contrast to the reforms set in motion by the silent advocate, sent ripples of disbelief and betrayal through the corridors. Olivia Sterling, grappling with the implications of the revelation, faced the challenge of navigating a complex web of fractured alliances. The news of Dr. Harris's implication hit Olivia Sterling like a tidal wave. The colleague she had once respected and collaborated with was now at the center of a scandal that jeopardized the reputation of the entire medical community. As the hospital teetered on the precipice of public scrutiny, Olivia Sterling found herself thrust into the role of mediator, investigator, and, reluctantly, judge. The fractures in alliances became immediately apparent. Colleagues who had once shared camaraderie and mutual respect now distanced themselves from Dr. Harris. Professional relationships built on trust and collaboration splintered as the shadows of doubt cast long, foreboding silhouettes over the once-cohesive medical community. The challenge for Olivia Sterling was twofold—she had to reconcile her own sense of betrayal while navigating the minefield of fractured alliances within the hospital. The once-unquestioned trust in her professional network now stood on shaky ground, and Olivia Sterling found herself questioning the authenticity of even the most enduring

Dreams in White Coats:

Dr. Olivia's Odyssey through Ten Healing Realms

relationships. In the days that followed the scandal's revelation, Olivia Sterling became an unintentional mediator between those who sought justice and those who clung to loyalty. The hospital, once a symbol of healing, became an arena where loyalties shifted like sand, and friendships were tested under the weight of ethical scrutiny. The fractures extended beyond the professional realm, seeping into the personal lives of those involved. Social gatherings once marked by laughter and shared victories now carried an air of tension and uncertainty. Olivia Sterling, caught in the crossfire of conflicting loyalties, found herself torn between her commitment to justice and the desire to salvage what remained of her fractured alliances. As she delved deeper into the investigation, Olivia Sterling discovered a tangled web of deceit and complicity that reached beyond Dr. Harris. The scandal, it seemed, was not an isolated incident but part of a broader pattern of ethical lapses within the medical community. The shadows of doubt threatened not only individual reputations but the very foundation of trust that held the profession together. The personal toll on Olivia Sterling was palpable. Her pursuit of justice strained relationships with colleagues she had once considered friends. The fractures widened as accusations flew, and alliances shifted based on allegiances and personal convictions. Olivia Sterling, caught in the storm, grappled with a profound sense of isolation as the once-unified front of the medical community splintered into factions. In a pivotal confrontation with Dr. Harris, Olivia Sterling sought answers to the questions that haunted her. The shadows of doubt that had eclipsed their once-shared ideals now loomed large, demanding an explanation and, perhaps, a semblance of closure. Dr. Harris, facing the consequences of his actions, offered no justification but instead a tacit acknowledgment of the irreversible damage caused. The fallout extended beyond the hospital's walls, attracting the attention of medical boards, regulatory bodies, and the media. The scandal, once confined to the shadows, became a public spectacle that further strained the already fractured alliances within the medical community. As the investigation progressed, Olivia Sterling faced the challenge of rebuilding trust within the medical community. The fractures, though irreparable in some cases, opened the door for a renewed commitment to ethical integrity. The silent advocate, once a lone voice in the pursuit of justice, found unexpected allies among those who shared her vision for a profession untarnished by the shadows of deceit. The journey through fractured alliances taught Olivia Sterling that resilience could emerge even from the shattered remnants of trust. The shadows of doubt, though persistent,

Dreams in White Coats:

Dr. Olivia's Odyssey through Ten Healing Realms

could be dispelled through transparency, accountability, and a collective commitment to ethical principles. The hospital, scarred but not irreparably damaged, became a crucible for transformation and renewal. As Olivia Sterling navigated the aftermath of the scandal, she emerged with a deeper understanding of the delicate dance between professional and personal alliances. The fractures, though painful, became catalysts for growth, forcing individuals within the medical community to confront their own ethical compass and reevaluate the foundations upon which their alliances were built. In the quiet moments of reflection, Olivia Sterling acknowledged the enduring strength that emerged from the crucible of fractured alliances. The journey, though tumultuous, had become a chapter in the ongoing narrative of resilience and transformation. The shadows of doubt, once menacing, had become a backdrop against which the unwavering commitment to ethical integrity shone even more brightly.

8 BREAKING POINT

The hospital, a place where healing and crisis coexisted, became a crucible that tested the limits of Olivia Sterling's resilience. The relentless demands of her medical responsibilities, combined with the weight of recent scandals and fractured alliances, pushed her to a breaking point. As the pressures mounted, Olivia Sterling found herself on the precipice of a personal crisis that would redefine her understanding of healing and humanity. The signs of strain were subtle at first—a lingering fatigue, a persistent sense of unease, and the gnawing feeling that the walls of responsibility were closing in. Olivia Sterling, driven by a deep sense of dedication to her patients, brushed aside the warning signals, attributing them to the inherent challenges of her profession. Little did she know that the universe had a life-altering event in store, a force that would challenge the very core of her beliefs. The breaking point arrived unexpectedly, embodied in a single phone call that shattered the fragile equilibrium of Olivia Sterling's life. Her mother, a pillar of strength and a source of unwavering support, had been diagnosed with a terminal illness. The news, a seismic shock that reverberated through Olivia Sterling's world, pushed her to confront the fragility of human existence in a way she had never anticipated. In the midst of the medical storm, Olivia Sterling found herself thrust into the role of both healer and grieving daughter. The relentless responsibilities of her profession, once a source of purpose, now became a suffocating weight that threatened to crush her. The hospital, a place of healing for others, became a battlefield where Olivia Sterling grappled with her own vulnerabilities and the looming inevitability of loss. As she juggled her duties within the hospital and the heartbreaking realities of her mother's illness, Olivia Sterling teetered on the edge of emotional exhaustion. The breaking point, elusive but inevitable, drew near as the delicate balance

Dreams in White Coats:

Dr. Olivia's Odyssey through Ten Healing Realms

between professional obligations and personal grief unraveled. The tipping point came during a particularly challenging day at the hospital. A patient, whose symptoms mirrored those of her mother, became the unwitting catalyst for Olivia Sterling's emotional unraveling. The shadows of loss and the relentless demands of her profession converged, pushing her to confront the painful truth that healing, despite her best efforts, was not always within her control. In the quiet sanctuary of her office, Olivia Sterling confronted her breaking point. The walls, once adorned with accolades and reminders of triumphs, now closed in on her, echoing the fragility of life. The weight of responsibility, coupled with the looming specter of personal loss, became an unbearable burden that threatened to extinguish the flame of resilience within her. In the depths of her crisis, Olivia Sterling discovered unexpected sources of solace. Colleagues, who had witnessed the toll of her silent struggle, offered gestures of support and understanding. The fractured alliances, once strained by scandal, now revealed their enduring strength as colleagues rallied to share the burden of her responsibilities. The hospital, which had been both a sanctuary and a battlefield, became a space where Olivia Sterling's vulnerability was met with compassion. The breaking point, though excruciating, became a crucible for transformation. In the midst of her personal crisis, Olivia Sterling found the resilience she needed in the unlikeliest of places—the shared humanity of those who understood the complexities of healing. As Olivia Sterling confronted her mother's illness and the inevitable loss that loomed on the horizon, she reevaluated the nature of healing. The once-clear boundaries between professional detachment and personal involvement blurred, revealing the interconnectedness of the healer's journey with the fragility of human existence. In the quiet moments by her mother's bedside, Olivia Sterling discovered the profound truth that healing, at its essence, was not always about curing but about providing solace, compassion, and a sense of shared humanity. The breaking point, once perceived as a threat to her resilience, became a gateway to a deeper understanding of the healing journey—one that transcended the confines of the hospital walls. In the final moments with her mother, Olivia Sterling faced the heart-wrenching reality of loss. The hospital, with its relentless demands and shadows of doubt, faded into the background as the fragility of life took center stage. In the midst of her grief, Olivia Sterling discovered a reservoir of strength—a resilience that transcended the breaking point and transformed into a profound acceptance of the inevitable cycles of life. As Olivia Sterling emerged from the crucible of her personal crisis,

Dreams in White Coats:

Dr. Olivia's Odyssey through Ten Healing Realms

she carried with her a renewed understanding of the healing journey. The hospital, once a stage for triumphs and challenges, became a backdrop against which the resilience of the human spirit and the interconnectedness of shared vulnerability shone even more brightly. The breaking point, though painful, became a catalyst for a profound transformation within Olivia Sterling. The lessons learned in the crucible of personal crisis reshaped her approach to healing, infusing her practice with a depth of empathy and understanding that transcended the boundaries of professional obligations. In the quiet aftermath of loss, Olivia Sterling emerged not as a broken healer but as a resilient soul, forever changed by the breaking point that had tested the limits of her humanity. The hospital, with its ever-shifting dynamics, remained a canvas for the ongoing journey of healing—one that embraced the complexities of life, loss, and the enduring strength that emerged from the crucible of vulnerability.

9 SHADOWS OF REDEMPTION

The echoes of loss lingered in the corridors of Olivia Sterling's life, intertwining with the challenges of her professional journey. The breaking point, though searing, became a crucible for transformation. As Olivia Sterling grappled with the aftermath of personal and professional upheaval, seeking redemption in the most unlikely of places, she encountered a patient whose mysterious ailment would serve as the catalyst for her own healing journey. The hospital, once a battlefield where Olivia Sterling confronted her breaking point, now held the promise of redemption. In the wake of her mother's passing, the shadows of grief clung to her like a relentless companion. The fractured alliances, the scandals, and the weight of responsibility still loomed, but within the hallowed halls of healing, Olivia Sterling sought solace and purpose. The patient, whose presence seemed almost serendipitous, arrived at the hospital with symptoms that defied conventional diagnosis. The mystery of the ailment echoed the uncertainty that shrouded Olivia Sterling's own life. In the shadows of this enigma, Olivia Sterling found an unexpected reservoir of strength and purpose—a pathway to redemption that unfolded within the intricate dance of healing. As Olivia Sterling delved into the complexities of the patient's case, the parallels between their journeys became increasingly apparent. The shadows of uncertainty that cloaked the patient mirrored the doubts that had besieged Olivia Sterling. The hospital, with its capacity for both crisis and redemption, became the stage where their destinies intertwined. The quest for answers, once driven by a sense of duty, now became a personal odyssey for Olivia Sterling. In the process, she rediscovered the essence of healing—a journey that extended beyond the confines of medical protocols and embraced the humanity that united patients and healers alike. Late nights

Dreams in White Coats:

Dr. Olivia's Odyssey through Ten Healing Realms

in the hospital, once a solitary pilgrimage through the corridors of grief, now transformed into shared moments of introspection and camaraderie with colleagues. The fractured alliances, though scarred, revealed a resilience that had weathered the storms of scandal. Olivia Sterling, navigating the shadows of redemption, found unexpected allies among those who had witnessed her journey of transformation. The patient, grappling with the mystery ailment, became more than a medical case; they became a reflection of the shared vulnerability inherent in the healing process. Olivia Sterling, no longer confined by the shadows of doubt and grief, embraced the opportunity to be a beacon of compassion for someone walking a path she had traversed. In the pursuit of answers, Olivia Sterling forged a deep connection with the patient. The hospital, a place where personal and professional boundaries blurred, became a sanctuary for healing and redemption. The shadows that had once threatened to engulf Olivia Sterling now served as a backdrop against which her resilience and compassion shone even more brightly. The breakthrough in the patient's diagnosis, when it came, was not just a triumph of medical expertise but a testament to the transformative power of empathy and shared humanity. The hospital, with its capacity for both suffering and redemption, became a haven where healing extended beyond the physical realm to touch the very core of the human spirit. As Olivia Sterling guided the patient through the shadows of uncertainty, she found herself on a parallel journey of redemption. The fractured alliances, scandals, and personal loss, once insurmountable obstacles, became stepping stones on the path to resilience. The hospital, with its ever-shifting dynamics, emerged as a sanctuary where compassion and purpose converged. In the quiet moments of reflection, Olivia Sterling acknowledged the profound shift that had occurred within her. The shadows of redemption, though born from personal and professional upheaval, had become a source of strength and purpose. The patient, once a mystery to be solved, had become a companion on the shared journey of healing. The impact of Olivia Sterling's transformative journey extended beyond the walls of the hospital. Colleagues, inspired by her resilience, began to view their profession through a lens of compassion rather than bureaucratic detachment. The scandals, now tempered by the shadows of redemption, served as cautionary tales rather than insurmountable obstacles. The patient, whose ailment had defied initial understanding, emerged from the shadows of uncertainty transformed and healed. In the process, Olivia Sterling discovered that redemption was not a destination but a continuous journey—a dance

Dreams in White Coats:

Dr. Olivia's Odyssey through Ten Healing Realms

between shadows and light, grief and joy, vulnerability and resilience. As Olivia Sterling emerged from the crucible of personal and professional challenges, the hospital, with its ever-evolving narratives, remained a testament to the enduring spirit of healing. The shadows of doubt, once menacing, had become allies in the journey of redemption. The fractures in alliances, scars that bore witness to the complexities of human relationships, became threads that wove a tapestry of resilience. The chapter of Shadows of Redemption unfolded, leaving behind a legacy of compassion and transformation. Olivia Sterling, no longer defined by the breaking point but shaped by the shadows she had confronted, continued her journey with a renewed sense of purpose. The hospital, a stage for the intricate dance of healing, stood as a beacon where redemption was not only possible but an integral part of the ongoing narrative of resilience and humanity

10 A HEALING LIGHT

As Olivia Sterling stood at the crossroads of her journey, the shadows of her past, present, and future converged in a poignant dance. The culmination of challenges, from personal grief to professional upheaval, led her to a profound revelation about the true essence of healing. In the final chapter, Olivia Sterling embarked on a transformative quest that transcended the boundaries of medicine, embracing the healing light within herself and becoming a beacon for others navigating the complex terrain of life, love, and medicine. The hospital, with its ever-shifting dynamics, remained the stage for Olivia Sterling's final reckoning with the shadows. The echoes of loss, scandals, and fractured alliances lingered, but she faced them with a newfound resilience born from the crucible of her experiences. The breaking point, the silent advocate, and the shadows of redemption had become chapters in a narrative that unfolded with both vulnerability and strength. In a quiet moment of reflection, Olivia Sterling confronted the shadows of her past—the traumatic incident that had haunted her, the loss of her mother, and the personal and professional challenges that had tested her resilience. It was within this sacred space of self-discovery that she unearthed a profound truth—the healing light existed within her, waiting to be acknowledged and embraced. The hospital, once a symbol of crisis and redemption, transformed into a sanctuary where Olivia Sterling sought not just to heal others but to illuminate the path to healing within herself. The challenges that had shaped her journey became stepping stones toward a deeper understanding of the interconnectedness of life, love, and the practice of medicine. As Olivia Sterling navigated the complexities of her present, she discovered that healing was not confined to medical protocols and diagnoses. The essence of healing lay in the ability to acknowledge one's

Dreams in White Coats:

Dr. Olivia's Odyssey through Ten Healing Realms

vulnerabilities, to confront the shadows within, and to extend compassion not only to patients but also to oneself. The fractured alliances, scars of past battles, became symbols of resilience and growth. The hospital, once a battleground of professional conflicts, now bore witness to a healer who had transcended the shadows to embody a healing light. Colleagues, inspired by her journey, began to view their roles not as mere practitioners of medicine but as compassionate guides in the intricate dance of life and healing. In the exploration of her future, Olivia Sterling glimpsed a horizon shaped by newfound wisdom. The hospital, with its revolving door of patients and challenges, became a canvas where she painted a legacy of compassion and transformation. The silent advocate's voice, once a lone echo, resonated in the collective consciousness of those who sought a deeper connection between medicine and the human spirit. The challenges that awaited Olivia Sterling in her future, though unknown, were embraced with a profound sense of purpose. The shadows that once threatened to engulf her now served as reminders of the ongoing dance between vulnerability and resilience, loss and growth. Olivia Sterling, having confronted the shadows within, stood on the threshold of a future illuminated by a healing light that radiated from the depths of her being. With each patient she encountered, Olivia Sterling became not just a healer of ailments but a guide through the shadows of human experience. The hospital, a microcosm of life's complexities, echoed with the resonance of her transformative journey. The breaking point, the silent advocate, the shadows of redemption—all converged into a tapestry that bore witness to the healing light that emanated from Olivia Sterling's soul. As the final chapter unfolded, Olivia Sterling emerged as a beacon for others navigating the complex terrain of life, love, and medicine. The hospital, a backdrop for the intricate dance of healing, became a testament to the enduring spirit of resilience and compassion. The shadows of doubt, once formidable, were dispelled by the radiant light of understanding and empathy. In the closing scenes of her journey, Olivia Sterling found solace in the quiet moments of connection with patients, colleagues, and the legacy she had woven within the hospital's walls. The healing light within her, once obscured by the shadows, now shone brightly, casting a warm glow on the lives she touched. As Olivia Sterling stepped into the unknown of her future, she carried with her the lessons learned from the challenges that shaped her. The hospital, with its ever-evolving narratives, stood as a living testament to the transformative power of resilience and compassion. Olivia Sterling, having confronted the

Dreams in White Coats:

Dr. Olivia's Odyssey through Ten Healing Realms

shadows of her past, present, and future, embraced the role of healer not as a mere profession but as a sacred calling—a conduit for the healing light that illuminated the intricate dance of life.

In the closing moments of her journey, Olivia Sterling found herself standing at the threshold of a future woven with threads of resilience, compassion, and the healing light she had discovered within. The hospital, a place that had witnessed her triumphs and tribulations, echoed with the whispers of countless stories, each a testament to the intertwining complexities of life and healing. With a heart brimming with gratitude, Olivia Sterling embraced the ever-shifting landscape of her profession. The breaking point, once a threat, had become the catalyst for transformation; the silent advocate had found a voice that resonated beyond the confines of the hospital; and the shadows of redemption had paved the way for a profound understanding of the healing journey. As Olivia Sterling continued her work, she carried the legacy of her experiences, not as burdens but as sacred offerings to the collective tapestry of humanity. The fractured alliances, scandals, and personal losses had become brushstrokes in a painting that depicted the intricate dance of life—fraught with shadows, yet illuminated by the healing light that emanated from within. In the quiet moments of reflection, Olivia Sterling realized that the true essence of healing transcended the boundaries of medicine. It was a dance that required an intimate connection with one's vulnerabilities, a compassionate acknowledgment of the shadows within, and an unwavering commitment to both the patient and the healer's own well-being. The hospital, a crucible of challenges and triumphs, continued to be a space where Olivia Sterling cultivated the healing light. Patients, once strangers seeking medical guidance, became companions on a shared journey of understanding and growth. Colleagues, inspired by her transformative journey, embraced a more compassionate approach to their practice. In the final scenes of this chapter, Olivia Sterling found herself surrounded by the echoes of gratitude and love—from patients who had found solace in her care, colleagues who had witnessed her unwavering commitment, and the legacy she had woven within the hospital's walls. The healing light, once a flicker in the shadows, had become a radiant beacon that illuminated the path for others to navigate their own healing journeys. As Olivia Sterling stepped into the embrace of the unknown future, she did so with a heart fortified by the resilience forged in the crucible of challenges. The shadows of her past, present, and future no longer held

Dreams in White Coats:

Dr. Olivia's Odyssey through Ten Healing Realms

the same ominous power; instead, they became markers of growth, compassion, and an enduring commitment to the sacred art of healing. In the final breaths of this narrative, Olivia Sterling's story became a testament to the profound wisdom that could emerge from the complexities of life. The healing light within her continued to shine, not just within the walls of the hospital but as a guiding force in the broader tapestry of existence. As the curtain fell on Olivia Sterling's journey, the hospital continued its ceaseless rhythm—a symphony of life, loss, and the unwavering pursuit of healing. The legacy she left behind was not just a collection of professional achievements but a reminder that, in the dance of shadows and light, each step forward brought with it the potential for transformation and the illumination of the healing light within us all.

ABOUT THE AUTHOR

Meet Wilfred Pool, the visionary author behind this compelling book. Drawing inspiration from the intersection of creativity and technology, Wilfred embarked on the journey of writing this book with a unique approach—collaborating with cutting-edge AI technology. Intrigued by the possibilities, Wilfred harnessed the power of AI, particularly the incredible assistance provided by the Amazon team, to bring his ideas to life. This collaboration opened new horizons, allowing Wilfred to explore innovative storytelling avenues and weave a narrative that captivates the imagination. Wilfred Pool's venture into the realm of AI-driven writing reflects his forward-thinking spirit and dedication to pushing the boundaries of traditional authorship. His ability to seamlessly integrate human creativity with technological innovation shines through in every page of this book. As an author who embraces the future of storytelling, Wilfred invites readers to join him on a literary journey where the synergy of human imagination and artificial intelligence creates a truly unique and immersive experience. With this book, Wilfred Pool leaves an indelible mark on the evolving landscape of modern literature, showcasing the endless possibilities that emerge when human creativity collaborates with the capabilities of advanced AI.

Made in the USA
Las Vegas, NV
26 January 2024